RICK RIORDAN
PRESENTS

READ THE
FIRST 2
CHAPTERS
OF THESE
3 BOOKS

Aru Shah
and the END of TIME

THE STORM RUNNER

DRAGON PEARL

CONTENTS

RICK RIORDAN PRESENTS

Aru Shah
AND THE END OF TIME

BY *NEW YORK TIMES* BEST-SELLING AUTHOR
ROSHANI CHOKSHI

Aru Shah
AND THE END OF TIME

A PANDAVA NOVEL

BOOK ONE

ROSHANI CHOKSHI

RICK RIORDAN PRESENTS

DISNEP • HYPERION   LOS ANGELES   NEW YORK

ISBN 978-1-368-01738-1

Visit www.DisneyBooks.com
Follow @ReadRiordan

SUSTAINABLE
FORESTRY
INITIATIVE
Certified Chain of Custody
Promoting Sustainable Forestry
www.sfiprogram.org
SFI-01054
The SFI label applies to the text stock

To my sisters:
Niv, Victoria, Bismah, Monica, and Shraya
We really need a theme song.

Aru Shah Is About to Explode Your Head

Have you ever read a book and thought, *Wow, I wish I'd written that!*?

For me, *Aru Shah and the End of Time* is one of those books. It has everything I like: humor, action, great characters, and, of course, awesome mythology! But this is not a book I could have written. I just don't have the expertise or the insider's knowledge to tackle the huge, incredible world of Hindu mythology, much less make it so fun and reader-friendly.

Fortunately for all of us, Roshani Chokshi does.

If you are not familiar with Hindu mythology—wow, are you in for a treat! You thought Zeus, Ares, and Apollo were wild? Wait until you meet Hanuman and Urvashi. You thought Riptide was a cool weapon? Check out this fine assortment of divine *astras*—maces, swords, bows, and nets woven from lightning. Take your pick. You're going to need them. You thought Medusa was scary? She's got nothing on the *nagini* and *rakshas*. Aru Shah, a salty and smart seventh-grade girl from Atlanta, is about to plunge into the midst of all this craziness, and her adventure will make your head explode in the best possible way.

If you already know Hindu mythology, you're about to have the most entertaining family reunion ever. You're going to see lots of your favorites—gods, demons, monsters, villains, and heroes. You're going to soar up to the heavens and down into the Underworld. And no matter how many of these myths you already know, I'll bet you a pack of Twizzlers you're going to learn something new.

Can you tell I'm excited to share this book with you? Yeah, I'm pretty excited.

So what are we waiting for? Aru Shah is hanging out in the Museum of Ancient Indian Art and Culture, where her mom works. Autumn break has started, and Aru is pretty sure it's going to be a boring day.

Yikes. She is SO wrong.

Rick Riordan

ONE

In Which Aru Regrets Opening the Door

The problem with growing up around highly dangerous things is that after a while you just get used to them.

For as long as she could remember, Aru had lived in the Museum of Ancient Indian Art and Culture. And she knew full well that the lamp at the end of the Hall of the Gods was not to be touched.

She could mention "the lamp of destruction" the way a pirate who had tamed a sea monster could casually say, *Oh, you mean ole Ralph here?* But even though she was used to the lamp, she had never once lit it. That would be against the rules. The rules she went over every Saturday, when she led the afternoon visitors' tour.

Some folks may not like the idea of working on a weekend, but it never felt like work to Aru.

It felt like a ceremony.

Like a secret.

She would don her crisp scarlet vest with its three honeybee buttons. She would imitate her mother's museum-curator voice, and people—this was the best part of all—would *listen*. Their eyes never left her face. Especially when she talked about the cursed lamp.

Sometimes she thought it was the most fascinating thing she ever discussed. A cursed lamp is a much more interesting topic than, say, a visit to the dentist. Although one could argue that both are cursed.

Aru had lived at the museum for so long, it kept no secrets from her. She had grown up reading and doing her homework beneath the giant stone elephant at the entrance. Often she'd fall asleep in the theater and wake up just before the crackling self-guided tour recording announced that India became independent from the British in 1947. She even regularly hid a stash of candy in the mouth of a four-hundred-year-old sea dragon statue (she'd named it Steve) in the west wing. Aru knew everything about everything in the museum. Except one thing…

The lamp. For the most part, it remained a mystery.

"It's not quite a lamp," her mother, renowned curator and archaeologist Dr. K. P. Shah, had told her the first time she showed it to Aru. "We call it a *diya*."

Aru remembered pressing her nose against the glass case, staring at the lump of clay. As far as cursed objects went, this was by far the most boring. It was shaped like a pinched hockey puck. Small markings, like bite marks, crimped the edges. And yet, for all its normal-ness, even the statues filling the Hall of the Gods seemed to lean away from the lamp, giving it a wide berth.

"Why can't we light it?" she had asked her mother.

Her mother hadn't met her gaze. "Sometimes light illuminates things that are better left in the dark. Besides, you never know who is watching."

Well, Aru had watched. She'd been watching her entire life.

Every day after school she would come home, hang her backpack from the stone elephant's trunk, and creep toward the Hall of the Gods.

It was the museum's most popular exhibit, filled with a hundred statues of various Hindu gods. Her mother had lined the walls with tall mirrors so visitors could see the artifacts from all angles. The mirrors were "vintage" (a word Aru had used when she traded Burton Prater a greenish penny for a whopping two dollars and half a Twix bar). Because of the tall crape myrtles and elms standing outside the windows, the light that filtered into the Hall of the Gods always looked a little muted. Feathered, almost. As if the statues were wearing crowns of light.

Aru would stand at the entrance, her gaze resting on her favorite statues—Lord Indra, the king of the heavens, wielding a thunderbolt; Lord Krishna, playing his flutes; the Buddha, sitting with his spine straight and legs folded in meditation—before her eyes would inevitably be drawn to the diya in its glass case.

She would stand there for minutes, waiting for something… anything that would make the next day at school more interesting, or make people notice that she, Aru Shah, wasn't just another seventh grader slouching through middle school, but someone *extraordinary*. . . .

Aru was waiting for magic.

And every day she was disappointed.

"Do something," she whispered to the god statues. It was a Monday morning, and she was still in her pajamas. "You've got plenty of time to do something awesome, because I'm on autumn break."

The statues did nothing.

Aru shrugged and looked out the window. The trees of Atlanta, Georgia, hadn't yet realized it was October. Only their top halves had taken on a scarlet-and-golden hue, as if someone had dunked them halfway in a bucket of fire and then plopped them back on the lawn.

As Aru had expected, the day was on its way to being uneventful. That should have been her first warning. The world has a tendency to trick people. It likes to make a day feel as bright and lazy as sun-warmed honey dripping down a jar as it waits until your guard is down....

And that's when it strikes.

Moments before the visitor alarm rang, Aru's mom had been gliding through the cramped two-bedroom apartment connected to the museum. She seemed to be reading three books at a time while also conversing on the phone in a language that sounded like a chorus of tiny bells. Aru, on the other hand, was lying upside down on the couch and pelting pieces of popcorn at her, trying to get her attention.

"Mom. Don't say anything if you can take me to the movies."

Her mom laughed gracefully into the phone. Aru scowled. Why couldn't *she* laugh like that? When Aru laughed, she sounded like she was choking on air.

"Mom. Don't say anything if we can get a dog. A Great Pyrenees. We can name him Beowoof!"

Now her mother was nodding with her eyes closed, which meant that she was *sincerely* paying attention. Just not to Aru.

"Mom. Don't say anything if I—"

Breeeeep!

Breeeeep!

Breeeeep!

Her mother lifted a delicate eyebrow and stared at Aru. *You know what to do.* Aru did know what to do. She just didn't want to do it.

She rolled off the couch and Spider-Man–crawled across the floor in one last bid to get her mother's attention. This was a difficult feat considering that the floor was littered with books and half-empty chai mugs. She looked back to see her mom jotting something on a notepad. Slouching, Aru opened the door and headed to the stairs.

Monday afternoons at the museum were quiet. Even Sherrilyn, the head of museum security and Aru's long-suffering babysitter on the weekends, didn't come in on Mondays. Any other day—except Sunday, when the museum was closed—Aru would help hand out visitor stickers. She would direct people to the various exhibits and point out where the bathrooms were. Once she'd even had the opportunity to yell at someone when they'd patted the stone elephant, which had a very distinct DO NOT TOUCH sign (in Aru's mind, this applied to everyone who wasn't her).

On Mondays she had come to expect occasional visitors seeking temporary shelter from bad weather. Or people who wanted to express their concern (in the gentlest way possible) that the Museum of Ancient Indian Art and Culture honored the devil. Or sometimes just the FedEx man needing a signature for a package.

What she did not expect when she opened the door to greet the new visitors was that they would be three students from Augustus Day School. Aru experienced one of those elevator-stopping-too-fast sensations. A low *whoosh* of panic hit her stomach as the three students stared down at her and her Spider-Man pajamas.

The first, Poppy Lopez, crossed her tan, freckled arms. Her brown hair was pulled back in a ballerina bun. The second, Burton Prater, held out his hand, where an ugly penny sat in his palm. Burton was short and pale, and his striped black-and-yellow shirt made him look like an unfortunate bumblebee. The third, Arielle Reddy—the prettiest girl in their class, with her dark brown skin and shiny black hair—simply glared.

"I knew it," said Poppy triumphantly. "You told everyone in math class that your mom was taking you to France for break."

That's what Mom had promised, Aru thought.

Last summer, Aru's mother had curled up on the couch, exhausted from another trip overseas. Right before she fell asleep, she had squeezed Aru's shoulder and said, *Perhaps I'll take you to Paris in the fall, Aru. There's a café along the Seine River where you can hear the stars come out before they dance in the night sky. We'll go to boulangeries and museums, sip coffee from tiny cups, and spend hours in the gardens.*

That night Aru had stayed awake dreaming of narrow winding streets and gardens so fancy that even their flowers looked haughty. With that promise in mind, Aru had cleaned her room and washed the dishes without complaint. And at school, the promise had become her armor. All the other students at Augustus Day School had vacation homes in places like the Maldives or Provence, and they complained when their yachts were under repair. The promise of Paris had brought Aru one tiny step closer to belonging.

Now, Aru tried not to shrink under Poppy's blue-eyed

gaze. "My mom had a top secret mission with the museum. She couldn't take me."

That was partly true. Her mom never took her on work trips.

Burton threw down the green penny. "You cheated me. I gave you two bucks!"

"And you got a *vintage* penny—" started Aru.

Arielle cut her off. "We know you're lying, Aru Shah. That's what you are: a *liar*. And when we go back to school, we're going to tell everyone—"

Aru's insides squished. When she'd started at Augustus Day School last month, she'd been hopeful. But that had been short-lived.

Unlike the other students, she didn't get driven to school in a sleek black car. She didn't have a home "offshore." She didn't have a study room or a sunroom, just *a* room, and even she knew that her room was really more like a closet with delusions of grandeur.

But what she did have was imagination. Aru had been day-dreaming her whole life. Every weekend, while she waited for her mom to come home, she would concoct a story: her mother was a spy, an ousted princess, a sorceress.

Her mom claimed she never wanted to go on business trips, but they were a necessity to keep the museum running. And when she came home and forgot about things—like Aru's chess games or choir practice—it wasn't because she didn't care, but because she was too busy juggling the state of war and peace and art.

So at Augustus Day School, whenever the other kids asked, Aru told tales. Like the ones she told herself. She talked about cities she'd never visited and meals she'd never eaten. If she arrived with scuffed-up shoes, it was because her old pair had been sent to Italy for repair. She'd mastered that delicate condescending eyebrow everyone else had, and she deliberately mispronounced the names of stores where she bought her clothes, like the French *Tar-Jay*, and the German *Vahl-Mahrt*. If that failed, she'd just sniff and say, "Trust me, you wouldn't recognize the brand."

And in this way, she had fit in.

For a while, the lies had worked. She'd even been invited to spend a weekend at the lake with Poppy and Arielle. But Aru had ruined everything the day she was caught sneaking from the car-pool line. Arielle had asked which car was hers. Aru pointed at one, and Arielle's smile turned thin. "That's funny. Because that's my driver's car."

Arielle was giving Aru that same sneer now.

"You told us you have an elephant," said Poppy.

Aru pointed at the stone elephant behind her. "I do!"

"You said that you rescued it from India!"

"Well, Mom said it was *salvaged* from a temple, which is fancy talk for *rescue*—"

"And you said you have a cursed lamp," said Arielle.

Aru saw the red light on Burton's phone: steady and unblinking. He was recording her! She panicked. What if the video went online? She had two possible choices: 1) She could hope the universe might take pity on her and allow her to burst into flames before homeroom, or 2) She could change her name, grow a beard, and move away.

Or, to avoid the situation entirely . . .

She could show them something impossible.

"The cursed lamp is real," she said. "I can prove it."

TWO

Oops

It was four p.m. when Aru and her three classmates walked together into the Hall of the Gods.

Four p.m. is like a basement. Wholly innocent in theory. But if you really think about a basement, it is cement poured over restless earth. It has smelly, unfinished spaces, and wooden beams that cast too-sharp shadows. It is something that says *almost, but not quite*. Four p.m. feels that way, too. Almost, but not quite afternoon anymore. Almost, but not quite evening yet. And it is the way of magic and nightmares to choose those almost-but-not-quite moments and wait.

"Where's your mom, anyway?" asked Poppy.

"In France," said Aru, trying to hold her chin up. "I couldn't go with her because I had to take care of the museum."

"She's probably lying again," said Burton.

"She's *definitely* lying. That's the only thing she's good at," said Arielle.

Aru wrapped her arms around herself. She was good at lots of things, if only people would notice. She was good at memorizing facts she had heard just once. She was good at chess, too, to the point where she might have gone to the state championship if Poppy and Arielle hadn't told her _Nobody joins chess, Aru. You can't do that._ And so Aru had quit the chess team. She used to be good at tests, too. But now, every time she sat down to take a test, all she could think of was how expensive the school was (it was costing her mom a fortune), and how everyone was judging her shoes, which were popular last year but not this year. Aru _wanted_ to be noticed. But she kept getting noticed for all the wrong reasons.

"I thought you said you had a condo downtown, but this dump was the address in the school directory," sniffed Arielle. "So you actually live _in_ a museum?"

Yep.

"No? Look around—do you see my room?"

It's upstairs. . . .

"If you don't live here, then why are you wearing pajamas?"

"Everyone wears pj's during the daytime in England," said Aru.

Maybe.

"It's what royalty does."

If I were royalty, I would.

"Whatever, Aru."

The four of them stood in the Hall of the Gods. Poppy wrinkled her nose. "Why do your gods have so many hands?"

The tops of Aru's ears turned red. "It's just how they are."

"Aren't there, like, a thousand gods?"

"I don't know," said Aru.

And this time she was telling the truth. Her mother had said that the Hindu gods were numerous, but they didn't stay as one person all the time. Sometimes they were reincarnated—their soul was reborn in someone else. Aru liked this idea. Sometimes she wondered who she might have been in another life. Maybe that version of Aru would have known how to vanquish the beast that was the seventh grade.

Her classmates ran through the Hall of the Gods. Poppy jutted out her hip, flicked her hands in imitation of one of the statues, then started laughing. Arielle pointed at the full-bodied curves of the goddesses and rolled her eyes. Heat crawled through Aru's stomach.

She wanted all the statues to shatter on the spot. She wished they weren't so . . . naked. So different.

It reminded her of last year, when her mother had taken her to the sixth-grade honors banquet at her old school. Aru had worn what she thought was her prettiest outfit: a bright blue *salwar kameez* flecked with tiny star-shaped mirrors and embroidered with thousands of silver threads. Her mother had worn a deep red sari. Aru had felt like part of a fairy tale. At least until the moment they had entered the banquet hall, and every gaze had looked too much like pity. Or embarrassment. One of the girls had loudly whispered, *Doesn't she know it isn't Halloween?* Aru had faked a stomachache to leave early.

"Stop it!" she said now, when Burton started poking at Lord Shiva's trident.

"Why?"

"Because . . . Because there are cameras! And when my mom comes back, she'll tell the government of India and they'll come after you."

Lie, lie, lie. But it worked. Burton stepped back.

"So where's this lamp?" asked Arielle.

Aru marched to the back of the exhibit. The glass case

winked in the early evening light. Beneath it, the diya looked wrapped in shadows. Dusty and dull.

"That's *it*?" said Poppy. "That looks like something my brother made in kindergarten."

"The museum acquired the Diya of Bharata after 1947, when India gained its independence from Britain," Aru said in her best impression of her mother's voice. "It is believed that the Lamp of Bharata once resided in the temple of"—*donotmispronounceKurekshetra*—"Koo-rook-shet-ra—"

"*Kooroo* what? Weird name. Why was it there?" asked Burton.

"Because that is the site of the Mahabharata War."

"The *what* war?"

Aru cleared her throat and went into museum attendant mode.

"The Mahabharata is one of two ancient poems. It was written in Sanskrit, an ancient Indic language that is no longer spoken." Aru paused for effect. "The Mahabharata tells the story of a civil war between the five Pandava brothers and their one hundred cousins—"

"One *hundred* cousins?" said Arielle. "That's impossible."

Aru ignored her.

"Legend says that lighting the Lamp of Bharata awakens the Sleeper, a demon who will summon Lord Shiva, the fearsome Lord of Destruction, who will dance upon the world and bring an end to Time."

"A dance?" scoffed Burton.

"A cosmic dance," said Aru, trying to make it sound better. When she thought of Lord Shiva dancing, she imagined someone stomping their feet on the sky. Cracks appearing in the clouds like lightning. The whole world breaking and splintering apart.

But it was clear her classmates were picturing someone doing the Cotton-Eyed Joe.

"So if you light the lamp, the world ends?" asked Burton.

Aru glanced at the lamp, as if it might consider contributing a few words. But it stayed silent, as lamps are wont to do. "Yes."

Arielle's lip curled. "So do it. If you're telling the truth, then do it."

"If I'm telling the truth—which I am, by the way—then do you have any idea what it could do?"

"Don't try to get out of this. Just light it once. I dare you."

Burton held up his phone. Its red light taunted her.

Aru swallowed. If her mom were down here, she would drag her away by the ears. But she was upstairs getting ready to go away—yet again. Honestly, if the lamp was so dangerous, then why keep leaving her alone with it? Yeah, Sherrilyn was there. But Sherrilyn spent most of the time watching *Real Housewives of Atlanta*.

Maybe it wouldn't be a big deal. She could just light a small flame, then blow it out. Or, instead, maybe she could break the glass case and act like she'd been cursed. She could start zombie-walking. Or Spider-Man–crawling. They'd all be scared enough never to talk about what had happened.

Please, oh, please, I'll never lie again, I promise.

She repeated this in her head as she reached for the glass case and lifted it. As soon as the glass was removed, thin red beams of light hit the lamp. If a single strand of hair fell on any of those laser beams, a police car would come rushing to the museum.

Poppy, Arielle, and Burton inhaled sharply at the same time. Aru felt smug. *See? I told you it was important.* She wondered if she could just stop there. Maybe this would be enough. And then Poppy leaned forward.

"Get it over with," she said. "I'm bored."

Aru punched in the security code—her birthday—and watched as the red beams disappeared. The air mingled with the scent of the clay diya. It smelled like the inside of a temple: all burnt things and spices.

"Just tell the truth, Aru," said Arielle. "If you do, all you have to do is pay us ten dollars each and we won't post the video of you getting caught in your own stupid lie."

But Aru knew that wouldn't be the end of it. Between a demon that could end the world and a seventh-grade girl, Aru (and probably most people) would choose the demon any day.

Without the red beams on it, the lamp felt dangerous. As if it had somehow sensed there was one less barrier. Cold stitched up Aru's spine, and her fingers felt numb. The small metal dish in the middle of the lamp looked a lot like an unblinking eye. Staring straight at her.

"I—I don't have a match," said Aru, taking a step back.

"I do." Poppy held out a green lighter. "I got it from my brother's car."

Aru reached for the lighter. She flicked the little metal wheel, and a tiny flame erupted. Her breath caught. *Just a quick light.* Then she could enact Plan Melodramatic Aru and get herself out of this mess and *never ever ever* lie again.

As she brought the flame closer to the lamp, the Hall of the Gods grew dark, as if a switch had turned off all the natural light. Poppy and Arielle moved closer. Burton tried to get closer, too, but Poppy shoved him away.

"Aru..."

A voice seemed to call out to her from *inside* the clay lamp.

She almost dropped the lighter, but her fist clenched around it just in time. She couldn't look away from the lamp. It seemed to pull her closer and closer.

"*Aru, Aru, Aru*—"

"Just get it over with, Shah!" screeched Arielle.

The red light on Burton's phone blinked in the corner of her vision. It promised a horrific year, cafeteria coleslaw in her locker, her mother's face crumpling in disappointment. But maybe if she did this, if by some stroke of luck she managed to trick Arielle and Poppy and Burton, maybe they'd let her sit beside them at lunch. Maybe she wouldn't have to hide behind her stories because her own life would finally be *enough*.

So she did it.

She brought the flame to the lip of the diya.

When her finger brushed the clay, a strange thought burst into Aru's head. She remembered watching a nature documentary about deep-sea creatures. How some of them used bait, like a glowing orb, to attract their prey. The moment a fish dared to swim toward the little light floating in the water, the sea creature would snatch it up with huge gaping jaws. That was how the lamp felt: a small halo of brightness held out by a monster crouching in the shadows....

A trick.

The moment the flame caught, light exploded behind Aru's eyes. A shadow unfurled from the lamp, its spine arching and reaching. It made a horrible sound—was that laughter? She couldn't shake the noise from her head. It clung to her thoughts like an oily residue. It was as if all the silence had been scraped off and thrown somewhere else.

Aru stumbled back as the shadow thing limped out of the lamp. Panic dug into her bones. She tried to blow out the candle, but the flame didn't budge. Slowly, the shadow grew into a nightmare. It was tall and spidery, horned and fanged and furred.

"Oh, Aru, Aru, Aru . . . what have you done?"

RICK RIORDAN PRESENTS

THE
STORM
RUNNER

J.C. CERVANTES

THE STORM RUNNER

J.C. CERVANTES

RICK RIORDAN PRESENTS

Disney • HYPERION   LOS ANGELES   NEW YORK

For Mom, my Seer
And for those who don't feel like they belong

WELCOME TO
THE VOLCANO

Zane Obispo has a pretty sweet life.

Since last year, he's been homeschooled, which means the other kids can't pick on him anymore. He gets to spend a lot of his time out in the desert of New Mexico, wandering and exploring with his faithful boxer-dalmatian, Rosie.

His mom loves him like crazy. His uncle Hondo is a fun housemate, even though he's maybe a little too addicted to pro wrestling and Flamin' Hot Cheetos.

As for the neighbors, Zane only has two: friendly Mr. Ortiz, who grows top secret chile-pepper varieties in his garden, and Ms. Cab, who works as a phone psychic and pays Zane to help her out. What's not to like?

And did I mention the volcano in Zane's backyard? That's right. Zane has his very own volcano. He and Rosie spend a lot of time climbing around on it. Recently, they even found a secret entrance that leads inside. . . .

Yep, life is good!

Er, except that Zane was born with mismatched legs. One has always been shorter than the other, so he walks with a limp and uses a cane. He's learning to deal, though, and is a crazy-fast hobbler.

Oh, and also...Zane just got accepted to a new private school. He doesn't want to go, but his mom is insisting. Class starts tomorrow.

Then there's the accident—Zane sees a small plane crash into the mouth of his volcano. He was close enough to glimpse the pilot's face...and either it was a very good Halloween mask, or the pilot was an alien zombie monster.

On top of all this, there's a pretty new girl in town—Brooks—who warns Zane he's in mortal danger. But Brooks doesn't exist, according to the school records. And how does she know who he is, anyway?

Soon, Zane discovers that nothing in his life is what he thought. There's a reason he was born with a limp. There's a reason he's never met his father—a mysterious guy his mom fell in love with on a trip to the Yucatán. Something very strange is going on in Zane's volcano, and Brooks claims it's all tied to some ancient prophecy.

How much do you know about the Maya myths? Did you know the Maya have a goddess of chocolate? (Dude, how come the Greeks don't get a goddess of chocolate? No fair.) The Maya also have shape-shifters, demons, magicians, giants, demigods, and an underworld that may or may not be accessible from the back of a local taco shop.

J. C. Cervantes is about to take you on a trip you will never forget, through the darkest, strangest, and funniest twists and turns of Maya myth. You will meet the scariest gods you can imagine, the creepiest denizens of the underworld, and the most amazing and unlikely heroes, who have to save our world from being ripped apart.

Maya myth and magic is closer than you think. In fact, it's right in our backyard.

Welcome to the volcano.

Welcome to *The Storm Runner*.

"Believing takes practice."
—Madeleine L'Engle

To Whom It May Concern,

Here it is. The story you forced me to write, with the details up to the bitter and unhappy end. All so I could serve as your poster boy for what happens when <u>anyone</u> defies the gods.

I never wanted any of this. But you didn't give me a choice. I ended up here because of some sacred oath I didn't even take, and because I made you so mad you wanted me dead.

I guess you got what you wanted.

Personally, I think you should be thanking me, but gods never show gratitude, do they?

I just want you to know I don't regret any of it. I'd do it all again, even knowing where I ended up. Okay, maybe I do have one regret—that I won't get to see your shocked faces when you read this. Anyhow, delivery made. See you on the other side.

Zane Obispo

1.

It all started when Mom screamed.

I thought she'd seen a scorpion, but when I got to the kitchen, she was waving a letter over her head and dancing in circles barefoot. After a year of being homeschooled, I was going to get to go to school again. Did you catch that word? *Get*. As in, someone was *allowing* me to learn. Stupid! Who put adults in charge, anyway? But here's the thing: I didn't want to go to some stuffy private school called Holy Ghost where nuns gave me the evil eye. And I for sure didn't want the Holy Ghost "shuttle" to come all the way out to no-man's-land to pick me up. Mine was the last stop, and that meant the van would probably be full when it arrived. And *full* meant at least a dozen eyes staring at me.

I smiled at Mom, because she looked happy. She took care of sick people in their homes all day, and she also let her brother, Hondo, live with us. He spent most of his time watching wrestling matches on TV and eating bags of Flamin' Hot Cheetos, so she didn't wear smiles too often.

"But . . ." I didn't know where to start. "You said I could be homeschooled."

"For a year," she said, still beaming. "That was the agreement. Remember? A single year."

Pretty sure that *wasn't* the agreement, but once something was in Mom's head, it was superglued there. Arguing was useless. Plus, I wanted her to be happy. Really, really happy. So I nodded hard and fast, because the harder I nodded, the more excited I'd look. I even threw in another smile.

"When?" It was September, and that meant I'd already missed a month of classes.

"You start tomorrow."

Crap!

"How about I start in January?" Yeah, you could say I was super optimistic.

Mom shook her head. "This is an incredible opportunity, Zane."

"Doesn't private school cost a lot?"

"They gave you a scholarship. Look!" She flashed the letter as proof.

Oh.

Mom folded the letter neatly. "You've been on the waiting list since . . ."

She didn't finish her sentence, but she didn't need to. *Since* referred to the day this jerk —a jerk whose face was seared into my brain—had mopped the floor with me at my old school, and I'd sworn never to set foot in any "place of learning" again.

"What about Ms. Cab?" I asked. "She needs my help. How am I going to pay for Rosie's food if I don't work?"

My neighbor, Ms. Cab (her real last name is Caballero, but I couldn't pronounce it as a little kid and the nickname stuck), was blind and needed an assistant to help her do stuff around the house. Also, she worked as a phone psychic, and

I answered the calls before she came on the line. It made her seem more legit. She paid me pretty good, enough to feed my dog, Rosie. Rosie was a boxmatian (half-boxer, half-dalmatian) and ate like an elephant.

"You can work in the afternoons." Mom took my hand in hers.

I hated when she did that during our arguments.

"Zane, honey, please. Things will be mejor this time. You're thirteen now. You need friends. You can't live out here alone with these..."

Out here was a narrow, dusty road in the New Mexico desert. Other than my two neighbors, there were tumbleweeds, rattlesnakes, coyotes, roadrunners, a dried-up riverbed, and even a dead volcano. But more on that later. Most people are surprised when they find out New Mexico has so many volcanoes. (Of course, *mine* was no ordinary act of nature, right, gods?)

"With these what?" I asked, even though I knew what she was thinking: *misfits.*

So what that Ms. Cab was a little different? And who cared that my other neighbor, Mr. Ortiz, grew weird varieties of chile peppers in his greenhouse? Didn't mean they were misfits.

"I'm just saying that you need to be with kids your age."

"But I don't like kids my age," I told her. "And I learn more without teachers."

She couldn't argue with that. I'd taught myself all sorts of things, like the generals of the Civil War, the number of blood vessels in the human body, and the names of stars and planets. That was the best thing about not going to school: I was the boss.

Mom ruffled my dark hair and sighed. "You're a genius, yes, but I don't like you hanging out only with a bunch of old people."

"Two isn't a bunch."

I guess I'd sort of been hoping Mom would forget our deal. Or maybe Holy Ghost (who named that school, anyway?) would disappear off the face of the earth in a freak cataclysmic accident.

"Mom." I got real serious and made her look me in the eyes. "No one wants to be friends with a freak." I tapped my cane on the ground twice. One of my legs was shorter than the other, which meant I walked with a dumb limp. It earned me all sorts of nicknames from the other kids: Sir Limps-a-Lot, McGimpster, Zane the Cane, and my all-time favorite: Uno—for the one good leg.

"You are *not* a freak, Zane, and . . ."

Oh boy. Her eyes got all watery like they were going to drown in her sadness.

"Okay, I'll go," I said, because I'd rather face a hundred hateful eyes than two crying ones.

She straightened, wiped her tears away with the back of her hand, and said, "Your uniform is pressed and waiting on your bed. Oh, and I have a present for you."

Notice how she dropped the bad news with something good? She should've run for mayor. There was no point in my griping about the uniform, even though the tie would probably give my neck a rash. Instead I decided to focus on the word *present*, and I held my breath, hoping it wasn't a rosary or something. Mom went to a cabinet and pulled out a skinny umbrella-size box with a silver ribbon tied around it.

"What is it?"

"Just open it." Her hands twitched with excitement.

I ripped open the box to get to the present that we didn't have money for. Inside was a wad of brown paper and under that, a shiny black wooden cane. It had a brass tip shaped like a dragon's head. "This is . . ." I blinked, searching for the right word.

"Do you like it?" Her smile could've lit up the whole world.

I turned the cane in my hands, testing its weight, and decided it looked like something a warrior would carry, which made it the coolest gift in the universe. "I bet it cost a lot."

Mom shook her head. "It was given to me. . . . Mr. Chang died last week, remember?"

Mr. Chang was a rich client who lived in a grande house in town and sent Mom home with chow mein every Tuesday. He was also a customer of Ms. Cab's—she was the one who'd gotten Mom the job to take care of him until he died. I hated to think of Mom hanging out with dying people, but as she always said, we had to eat. I'd tried eating less, but that was getting harder and harder the older I got. I'd already reached a whopping five foot nine. That made me the tallest in my family.

I ran my hands over the brass dragon head with the flames flying out of its mouth.

"He collected all sorts of things," Mom continued. "And his daughter said I should have this. She knew you—" She stopped herself. "She said the dragon symbolizes protection."

So Mom thought I needed protection. That made me feel pretty miserable. But I knew she meant well.

I rested my weight against it. It felt perfect, like it was made for me. I was excited to cruise around with this much cooler cane instead of my dumb plain brown one that screamed *I'm a freak*. "Thanks, Mom. I really like it."

"I thought it would make going back to school . . . easier," Mom said.

Right. Easier. Nothing, not even this warrior dragon cane, was going to make my being the new kid any easier.

It was a low point, and I didn't think things could get any worse. But boy, was I wrong.

That night, as I lay in bed, I thought about the next day. My stomach was all twisted in knots, and I wished I could turn into primordial ooze and seep into the ground. Rosie knew something was up, because she let out little groans and nuzzled her head against my hand, soft-like. I petted the white patch between her eyes in small circles.

"I know, girl," I whispered. "But Mom looked so happy."

I wondered what my dad would say about the whole thing. Not that I'd ever know—I'd never even met the guy. He and Mom hadn't gotten married, and he'd bounced before I was born. She'd only told me three things about him: He was superbly handsome (her words, not mine). He was from Mexico's Yucatán region. (She'd spent time there before I was born and said the sea is like glass.) And the third thing? She loved him to pieces. Whatever.

It was all quiet, except for the crickets and my guts churning. I clicked on the lamp and sat up.

On my nightstand was the Maya mythology book Mom had given me for my eighth birthday. It was part of a five-volume set about Mexico, but this book was the coolest. I figured it was her way of showing me my dad's culture without having to talk about him. The book had a tattered green cover with big gold letters on it: *The Myths and Magic of the Maya*. It was filled with color illustrations and stories about the adventures of different gods, kings, and heroes. The gods sounded awesome, but authors lie all the time.

I opened the book. On the endpapers was an illustration of a Maya death mask made of crumbling jade, with squinted lidless eyes and square stone teeth like tiny gravestones.

I swear the face was smiling at me.

"What're you looking at?" I huffed, slamming the book closed.

I tossed off the covers, got up, and peered out the window. It was all shadows and silence. There was only one good thing about living on the mesa: it was a hundred yards from a dead volcano (aka the Beast).

Having my own volcano was about the most interesting thing in my short life. (Up until that point, that is.) I'd even found a secret entrance into it last month. Rosie and I were hiking down from the top, and about halfway down I heard a strangled gasp. Naturally, I went to investigate, half expecting to find a hurt animal. But when I parted the scraggly creosote branches, I discovered something else: an opening just big enough to crawl through. It led to a whole labyrinth of caves, and for half a second I'd thought about calling *National Geographic* or something. But then I'd decided I would rather have a private place for Rosie and me than be on the cover of some dumb magazine.

Rosie leaped off the bed when she saw me slip on my sneakers.

"Come on, girl. Let's get out of here."

I went outside with my new warrior cane and limped past Nana's grave (she died when I was two, so I didn't remember her). I crossed the big stretch of desert, zigzagging between creosote, ocotillo, and yucca. The moon looked like a huge fish eye.

"Maybe I could just *pretend* to go to school," I said to Rosie as we got closer to the Beast, a black cone rising a couple hundred yards out of the sand to meet the sky.

Rosie stopped, sniffed the air. Her ears pricked.

"Okay, fine. Bad idea. You have a better one?"

With a whimper, Rosie inched back.

"You smell something?" I said, hoping it wasn't a rattlesnake. I hated snakes. When I didn't hear the familiar rattling, I relaxed. "You're not afraid of another jackrabbit, are you?"

Rosie yelped at me.

"You *were* afraid, don't try to deny it."

She took off toward the volcano. "Hey!" I called, trying to keep up. "Wait for me!"

I'd found Rosie wandering the desert four years ago. At the time, I figured someone had dumped her there. She was all skin and bones, and she acted skittish at first, like someone had abused her. When I begged Mom to let me keep her, she said we couldn't afford it, so I promised to earn money for dog food. Rosie was cinnamon brown like most boxers, but she had black spots all over, including on her floppy ears, which is why I was sure she had dalmatian in her, too. She only had three legs, so she got me and I got her.

When we got to the base of my volcano, I stopped abruptly. There, in the moonlit sand, was a series of paw prints—massive, with long claws. I stepped into one of the impressions and my size-twelve foot took up only a third of the space. The paw was definitely too big to belong to a coyote. I thought maybe they were bear tracks, except bears don't cruise the desert.

I kneeled to investigate. Even without the moonlight I would've been able to see the huge prints, because I had perfect eyesight in the dark. Mom called it a sacred ancestral blessing. Whatever. I called it another freak-of-nature thing.

"They look big enough to belong to a dinosaur, Rosie."

She sniffed one, then another, and whimpered.

I followed the trail, but it ended suddenly, like whatever creature the prints belonged to had simply vanished. Shivers crept up my spine.

Rosie whimpered again, looking up at me with her soft brown eyes as if to say *Let's get outta here.*

"Okay, okay," I said, just as eager as she was to get to the top of the volcano.

We climbed the switchback trail, past my secret cave (which I'd camouflaged with a net of creosote and mesquite branches), toward the ridge.

When we got to the top, I took in the jaw-dropping view. To the east was a glittering night sky rolling over the desert, and to the west was a lush valley dividing the city and the flat mesa. And beyond that? A looming mountain range with jagged peaks that stood shoulder to shoulder like a band of soldiers.

This was pretty much my favorite place in the world. Not that I'd ever been outside New Mexico, but I read a lot. Mom always told me the volcano was unsafe, without ever really saying why, but to me it had always felt quiet and calm. It also happened to be where I trained. After the docs had said there was no way to fix my bum leg, I spent hours hiking the Beast, thinking if I could just make my shorter leg stronger, maybe my limp would be less noticeable.

No such luck. But by walking the rim's edge I learned how to be a boss at balancing, and that's a handy skill when you get shoved around by kids at school.

I set down my cane and began teetering along the rim of the crater while holding my arms out to my sides. Mom would kill me if she knew I did this. One slip and I'd tumble fifty feet down the rocky hill.

Rosie cruised behind me, sniffing the ground.

"How 'bout I pretend to be sick?" I said, still stuck on how to get out of Holy Ghost school. "Or I could release rats into the cafeteria. . . . There can't be school if there's no food, right?" Did Catholic schools even have a cafeteria? The only problem was, my ideas would only buy me a day or two.

A low rumble rolled across the sky.

Rosie and I both stopped in our tracks and looked up. A small aircraft zoomed over the Beast, turned, and came back.

I stepped away from the crater's edge, craning my neck to get a better look.

I waved, hoping the pilot could see me. But he didn't come near enough. Instead, he started zigzagging like a crazy person. I thought maybe he was borracho until he circled back perfectly for another run. This time he came in tighter. Just when I thought the pilot was going to pull up, he pointed the plane's nose toward the center of the crater. The wings were so close to me I could practically see the screws holding them together. The plane's thrust shook the ground, sending me stumbling, but I caught myself.

Then something started glowing inside the cockpit. An eerie yellowish-blue light. Except what I saw had to have been some kind of a hallucination or optical illusion, because there was no pilot—there was a *thing*. An alien head thing with red bulging eyes, no nose, and a mouth filled with long sharp fangs. Yeah, that's right. An alien demon dude was flying the plane right into the Beast's mouth! Everything happened in sickeningly slow motion. I heard a crash, and a fiery explosion rocked the world, big enough to make even the planets shake.

I did a drop roll as flames burst from the top of the volcano. Rosie yelped.

"Rosie!"

And before I knew it I was tumbling down, down, down away from the Beast, away from my dog, and away from life as I knew it.

2

..

When I opened my eyes, the sky was a sea of black and the world was muffled, like I had cotton balls stuffed in my ears.

I rolled over with a groan and saw that I'd tumbled about twenty yards down from the rim. My head was pounding and, after a quick inventory, I found two scraped wrists and a bleeding elbow. Then I remembered: Rosie! Where was she?

I got to my feet, frantically scanning the dark. "Rosie! Come on, girl." I was about to climb back up to the top, when I thought I heard her cry near the base. "Rosie!" Quickly, I hobbled to the bottom of the trail, feeling woozy and light-headed.

When I got there, I squatted to catch my breath. That's when Mom showed up. She fell to her knees in front of me and death-gripped my shoulders. Her eyes were flooded with tears and she was spitting out all kinds of Spanish—mostly "Gracias a Dios"—which she always did when she was freaked.

"I heard the explosion!" she cried. "I went to check on you and you weren't in your bed and"—she gripped me tighter—"I told you *not* to come out here. Especially at night. What were you thinking?"

"I'm okay," I said, slipping onto my butt. I looked up at the Beast, blacker than a desert beetle. How long had I been knocked out? "Have you seen Rosie?" I asked hopefully.

But Mom didn't answer. She was too busy thanking the saints and squeezing me.

My heart started to jackhammer against my chest in a terrible panic. "Mom!" I shrugged her off me. "Where is she?"

A second later, Rosie was there with my cane tucked in her mouth. I took it from her and she began licking my face and pawing me like she was making sure I was really alive. I pulled my dog to me, hugging her broad chest, burying my face in her neck so Mom wouldn't see the tears forming. "I love you, you stupid, stupid dog," I whispered so only Rosie could hear.

It didn't take long for the ambulance, cops, fire trucks, and camera crews to show up. Was everyone here just for me? Then I remembered the creepy guy who had crashed. He definitely needed more help than I did. Within a few minutes the paramedics checked me out, bandaged my cuts, and told Mom I had a bump on the head and should get a CT scan. That sounded expensive.

"I'm fine," I said, standing to prove it.

I could read the paramedic's doubtful elevator eyes taking me in and stopping on my cane.

"I've got a straw leg," I told him, leaning against my cane, thinking that sounded better than *freak leg*.

Mom shook her head.

"What's wrong with your leg?" the paramedic asked.

"His right leg just hasn't caught up with the left one yet," she said.

The truth was, nobody knew. Not a single doctor had been able to tell us "definitively" why my leg hadn't grown properly, which meant I could probably be on one of those medical mystery shows if I wanted to. I'd for sure rather be a mystery than a definition.

I was glad Mom didn't say anything about my right *foot*. It was two sizes smaller than my left one, which was why Mom always had to buy two stupid pairs of shoes every time I wore out a pair.

The cops were next. After I told Officer Smart (real name, no lie) what happened, she said, "So the plane just crashed into the crater."

I nodded, keeping a tight grip on Rosie, who was dancing in place and whining as she stared at the volcano. "We're safe now, girl," I told her in a low voice.

Smart continued with the questions. "Did the plane look like it was in trouble? Did it make any weird sounds? Was there any smoke?"

I shook my head. There'd been no signs of distress, but I recalled the pilot's glowing red eyes and long fangs. I must have imagined them. . . .

"Well?" Officer Smart asked.

"I don't remember." The less I said, the better. If I told them what I'd seen, they'd really think I needed a head scan. "What happened to the pilot?" I had to ask.

Smart glanced at Mom like she was looking for permission to tell me the awful truth.

"We haven't found anyone," Smart said. "There's a search crew on the way."

I didn't see how anyone could have survived crashing into . . . *Hold on. Search crew?* My body stiffened. What if they found my cave? It would be all over the news and all kinds of explorers would show up, thinking it was *their* volcano.

A car pulled up, and a second later Mr. O and Ms. Cab got out. They crossed the night desert slowly. She was wearing her big Chanel sunglasses to cover her nonworking eyes, and he had on his wide-brimmed cowboy hat, as usual, to cover his baldness. They looked like an old married couple, but unfortunately for Mr. O, that wasn't the case. He was always asking me questions about her: *What's her favorite color? Does she ever talk about me? Do you think she'd go out with me?* So one day I finally asked Ms. Cab if she'd ever be Mr. O's girlfriend. By the look she gave me, you'd think I had asked her to leap into a fire pit. I never told Mr. O about it, because I knew it would make him feel fatter and balder than he already did, and he hadn't given up. He was always working on some scheme to get her to go out to dinner with him. I respected the guy for that.

"Zane!" Mr. O said as he led Ms. Cab by the arm. His brown eyes were huge with worry. "I saw the explosion. Are you okay? Did the fire catched you?"

"It's *catch*," Ms. Cab mumbled as she pushed her glasses up the bridge of her nose.

I must've drop-rolled just in time, I thought.

Mom patted my shoulders. "Thank the saints, he's safe now."

"No good comes from stepping out of your house in the middle of the night, Zane," Ms. Cab said. "What were you thinking?" She turned her head toward the volcano, and even behind her sunglasses, I could see her scowl. Her hands went to the Maya jade pendant dangling from a leather cord around her neck. She'd told me once that a protector spirit lived inside the jade. Seemed a pretty lame (and claustrophobic) place to live.

Smart asked to speak alone to Mom, and they wandered out of earshot.

Before I could wonder what that was about, Ms. Cab took me aside. "I've told you, this place is muy peligroso. You shouldn't spend time here."

"It's not dangerous," I argued. *At least it wasn't before tonight,* I thought.

"Evil lurks here, Zane." Ms. Cab adjusted her sunglasses. "I can sense it. You must stay away."

Ha. If she only knew I'd found a way inside! Good thing her psychic abilities were hit-and-miss. It would seriously stink if she could see *everything.*

"Did you predict the plane crash?" I asked. "Did you know it was going to happen?"

Rosie chose that moment to break free. She took off running toward the volcano. Even with only three legs, she was a little rocket. I went after her, taking long strides, wishing I could break into a run. Still, I was a crazy-fast hobbler. "Rosie!"

"Zane!" Mom called after me.

I jumped from shadow to shadow to slip past the searchers. I headed around to the other side of the mountain, in the direction Rosie had gone. When I got there, the coast was clear—no one else was nosing around there yet. Smoke curled from the top of the Beast as if it were awake. Rosie stood at the base, barking like crazy. I picked my way toward her, wondering what had gotten her so worked up, and was finally able to grab her collar. Then my eyes followed hers until I saw what she saw.

I didn't think I'd hit my head *that* hard. I froze, thinking what I was seeing had to be a hallucination.

I still wasn't sure what exactly had been in the cockpit when the plane was coming straight toward me: An alien? A monster? A drunk pilot in a really good Halloween costume? Whatever *it* was, it had to have been killed in that crash. Yet here the dude was, behind a scrub brush a mere twenty feet in front of me, hunched over and digging like a wild animal. In the flesh, it was even more hideous than before, and it for sure wasn't an alien or an award-winning costume. It . . . it looked like one of the monsters from my mythology book, except this guy was a whole lot uglier. The monster's skin was a pasty bluish gray in the moonlight. It didn't wear any clothes, but it didn't need any. Its bloated body was covered in patches of dark hair. Cauliflower-like ears drooped down to its bulging neck. It turned and looked at me straight on with its huge lidless eyes. Standing up to its full freakish ten-foot height, it hobbled toward me, dragging its knuckles across the ground. How the heck had this dude fit in that tiny plane?

It hissed something at me that sounded like *Ah-pooch*. Or maybe it was *Ah, puke*. My mind was reeling too much to be sure.

I opened my mouth to scream, but nothing came out.

A giant black owl with glowing yellow eyes circled just a few feet above my head. It swooped so low, I had to duck to avoid its talons.

Mom caught up with me then. "Zane, what's wrong with you? Why did you run off like that?"

"Mom, get back!" Why wasn't she screaming?

The monster opened its awful mouth and yellow slime oozed out.

Rosie howled like a banshee. I gripped my cane, ready to stab the thing in the eye. Anything to keep it away from Mom.

In the same moment, the monster groaned and disappeared into a thin trail of smoke that curled into the sky.

My heart double-punched my ribs. "Did . . . did you see it?"

"See what?" Mom felt my forehead. "You're scaring me, Zane. Maybe we should get that scan."

"I'm fine. Really. It was just . . . a coyote."

Except I wasn't fine. Not even close.

I patted Rosie to calm her—no, both of us—down. At least my dog had seen the monster, too. But why hadn't Mom?

"Necesitas rest," she said. "Let's get you to bed."

The second my mom left my bedroom, I checked my Maya book. I found an illustration that looked pretty close to the creature, down to the hairy knuckles and bulging eyes. I read the caption twice to be sure. "A demon of Xib'alb'a, the underworld," I whispered to Rosie. "But how can that be? These are just stories, not real life. . . ."

She pawed my leg and whimpered.

"Yeah, I'm creeped out, too, girl."

I slid the book beneath my bed and hopped under the covers. Rosie groaned.

"Right. Get rid of it."

I retrieved the book, then got up and went to my dresser, where Mom made me keep a vial of holy water. I splashed some on the picture of the demon, then shoved the book under a pile of dirty clothes in my closet and shut the door.

Once I was back in bed, Rosie settled against me and I could feel her heartbeat thudding, telling me she was still scared.

It was impossible to fall asleep. Seeing the plane crash had been terrible, and thinking Rosie could've been burned was pretty bad, too. Seeing that evil thing had been . . . well, beyond horrible.

And then there was the weirdness with Mom. Why hadn't she been able see the demon, too? *What if it had attacked us?* I wondered. *Could Rosie and I have protected her?*

I squeezed my eyes closed, but I couldn't escape the terrifying image.

But something else terrified me even more: knowing that with my bum leg I'd never be able to run fast enough to escape the monster.

RICK RIORDAN PRESENTS

DRAGON PEARL

YOON HA LEE

DRAGON PEARL

YOON HA LEE

RICK RIORDAN PRESENTS

Disney · HYPERION   LOS ANGELES   NEW YORK

This one is for Arabelle Sophie Betzwieser,
my favorite Dragon

A THOUSAND
DANGEROUS WORLDS

Min is just your average teenaged fox spirit, living with her family on the dusty backwater planet of Jinju.

Oh, sure, like all foxes, she can shape-shift into whatever she wants: human, animal, even a dining room table. And yes, she has the power to Charm—to manipulate human emotions and make people see things that aren't there. But that's not very exciting when you're stuck in a small dome house, sleeping every night in a crowded common room with your snoring cousins, spending every day fixing condensers in the hydroponics unit. Min yearns to join the Space Forces like her older brother Jun did—to see the Thousand Worlds and have marvelous adventures!

It's not like her mom will let her use magic anyway. Unlike other supernaturals, such as dragons, who can control weather, and goblins, who can conjure things out of thin air, fox spirits have a bad reputation. According to the old lore, foxes used to change shape to trick and prey on humans. Min's family wouldn't even consider doing such a thing, but due to lasting prejudice, they have to hide their true nature.

One day, an investigator from the government pays a visit to her mom. He brings horrible news: Jun has disappeared. Worse, Jun is suspected of treason—of abandoning his post to search for a fabled relic that has the power to transform worlds: the Dragon Pearl.

Min knows that Jun would never desert the Space Forces. Something must have happened to him. He needs help! Unfortunately, nobody seems interested in what Min thinks, especially after she knocks the investigator unconscious for insulting her brother's honor. Her family decides to ship her off to the boondocks to keep her out of further trouble, but Min has other ideas. She runs away from home, intent on following Jun to the stars. One young fox spirit, alone against the galaxies, will risk everything to find her brother and discover the mystery of the long-lost Dragon Pearl.

Buckle up, fellow foxes. Get ready for epic space battles. Prepare yourselves for magic and lasers, ghosts and dragons, interstellar pirates and warlike tigers. The Thousand Worlds hold all sorts of danger, but there are also priceless magical treasures to be discovered. And if Min succeeds, she might not only save her brother—she might save her entire planet.

Dragon Pearl will be like nothing you've ever read: a zesty mix of Korean folklore, magic, and science fiction that will leave you *longing* for more adventures in the Thousand Worlds!

Rick Riordan

ONE

I almost missed the stranger's visit that morning.

I liked to sleep in, though I didn't get to do it often. Waking up meant waking early. Even on the days I had lessons, my mom and aunties loaded me down with chores to do first. Scrubbing the hydroponics units next to our dome house. Scrounging breakfast from our few sad vegetables and making sure they were seasoned well enough to satisfy my four aunties. Ensuring that the air filters weren't clogged with the dust that got into everything.

I had a pretty dismal life on Jinju. I was counting the days until I turned fifteen. Just two more years left before I could take the entrance exams for the Thousand Worlds Space Forces and follow my brother, Jun, into the service. That was all that kept me going.

The day the stranger came, though—that day was different.

I was curled under my threadbare blanket, stubbornly clinging to sleep even though light had begun to steal in through the windows. Then my oldest cousin Bora's snoring got too loud to ignore. I often wished I had a room of my own, instead of sharing one with three cousins. Especially since Bora snored like a dragon. I kicked her in the side. She grunted but didn't stir.

We all slept on the same shabby quilt, handed down from my ancestors, some of the planet's first settlers. The embroidery had once depicted magpies and flowers, good-luck symbols. Most of the threads had come loose over the years, rendering the pictures illegible. When I was younger, I'd asked my mom why she didn't use Charm to restore it. She'd given me a stern look, then explained that she'd have to redo it every day as the magic wore off—objects weren't as susceptible to Charm as people were. I'd shut up fast, because I didn't want her to add that chore to my daily roster. Fortunately, my mom disapproved of Charm in general, so it hadn't gone any further.

All my life I'd been cautioned not to show off the fox magic that was our heritage. We lived disguised as humans and rarely used our abilities to shape-shift or Charm people. Mom insisted that we behave as proper, civilized foxes so we wouldn't get in trouble with our fellow steaders, planet-bound residents of Jinju. In the old days, foxes had played tricks like changing into beautiful humans to lure lonely travelers close so they could suck out their lives. But our family didn't do that.

The lasting prejudice against us annoyed me. Other supernaturals, like dragons and goblins and shamans, could wield their magic openly, and were even praised for it. Dragons used their weather magic for agriculture and the time-consuming work of terraforming planets. Goblins, with their invisibility caps, could act as secret agents; their ability to summon food with their magical wands came in handy, too. Shamans were essential for communicating with the ancestors and spirits, of course. We foxes, though—we had never overcome our bad reputation. At least most people thought we were extinct nowadays.

I didn't see what the big deal was about using our powers

around the house. We rarely had company—few travelers came to the world of Jinju. According to legend, about two hundred years ago, a shaman was supposed to have finished terraforming our planet with the Dragon Pearl, a mystical orb with the ability to create life. But on the way here, both she and the Pearl had disappeared. I didn't know if anything in that story was true or not. All I knew was that Jinju had remained poor and neglected by the Dragon Council for generations.

As I reluctantly let go of sleep that morning, I heard the voice of a stranger in the other room. At first I thought one of the adults was watching a holo show—maybe galactic news from the Pearled Halls—and had the volume turned up too high. We were always getting reports about raids from the Jeweled Worlds and the Space Forces' heroic efforts to defend us from the marauders, even if Jinju was too far from the border to suffer such attacks. But the sound from our holo unit always came out staticky. No static accompanied this voice.

It didn't belong to any of the neighbors, either. I knew everyone who lived within an hour's scooter ride. And it wasn't just the unfamiliarity of the voice, deep and smooth, that made me sit up and take notice. No one in our community spoke that formally.

Were we in trouble with the authorities? Had someone discovered that fox spirits weren't a myth after all? The stranger's voice triggered my old childhood fears of our getting caught.

"You must be misinformed." That was Mom talking. She sounded tense.

Now I really started to worry.

". . . no mistake," the voice was saying.

No mistake what? I had to find out more.

I slipped out from under the blanket, freezing in place when

Bora grunted and flopped over. I bet starship engines made less racket. But if the stranger had heard Bora's obnoxious noises, he gave no sign of it.

I risked a touch of Charm to make myself plainer, drabber, harder to see. Foxes can smell each other's magic—one of my aunties described the sensation as being like a sneeze that won't come out—but my mom might be distracted enough not to notice.

"How is this possible?" I heard Mom ask.

My hackles rose. She was clearly distressed, and I'd never known her to show weakness in front of strangers.

I tiptoed out of the bedroom and poked my head around the corner. There stood Mom, small but straight-backed. And then came the second surprise. I bit down on a sneeze.

Mom was using Charm. Not a lot—just enough to cover the patches in her trousers and the wrinkles in her worn shirt, and to restore their color to a richer green. We hadn't expected visitors, especially anybody important. She wouldn't have had time to dress up in the fine clothes she saved for special occasions. It figured she'd made an exception for herself to use fox magic, despite the fact that she chastised me whenever I experimented with it.

The stranger loomed over her. I didn't smell any Charm on him, but he could have been some other kind of supernatural, like a tiger or a goblin, in disguise. It was often hard to tell. I sniffed more closely, hoping to catch a whiff of emotion. Was he angry? Frustrated? Did he detect Mom's magic at all? But he held himself under such tight control that I couldn't get a bead on him.

His clothes, finely tailored in a burnished-bronze-colored fabric, were all real. What caught my eye was the badge on the breast of his coat. It marked him as an official investigator of the Thousand Worlds, the league to which Jinju belonged. There weren't literally a thousand planets in the league, but it encompassed many star systems, all answering to the same government. I'd never been off-world myself, although I'd often dreamed of it. This man might have visited dozens of worlds for his job, even the government seat at the Pearled Halls, and I envied him for it.

More to the point, what was an investigator doing here? I could only think of one thing: something had happened to my brother, Jun. My heart thumped so loudly I was sure he and Mom would hear it.

"Your son vanished under mysterious circumstances," the investigator said. "He is under suspicion of desertion."

I gasped involuntarily. Jun? Deserting?

"That's impossible!" Mom said vehemently. "My son worked very hard to get into the Space Forces!" I didn't need my nose to tell me how freaked-out she was.

I remembered the way Jun's face had lit up when he'd gotten the letter admitting him to the Academy. It had meant everything to him—he would never run off! I bit the side of my mouth to keep from blurting that out.

The investigator's eyes narrowed. "That may be, but people change, especially when they are presented with certain . . . *opportunities*."

"Opportunities . . . ?" Mom swallowed and then asked in a small voice, "What do you mean?"

"According to his captain's report, your son left to go in search of the Dragon Pearl."

I wasn't sure which stunned me more: the idea of Jun leaving the Space Forces, or the fact that the Dragon Pearl might actually exist.

"The Pearl? How...?" my mother asked incredulously. "No one knows where it—"

"The Dragon Council has made strides in locating it," the investigator said, rudely cutting her off. "And they would pay handsomely to have it back in their possession. If he found it, your son could have found the temptation irresistible...."

No. I knew my brother wouldn't risk his career by trying to cash in an artifact, even one as renowned as the Dragon Pearl.

Mom's shoulders slumped. I wanted to tell her not to believe the investigator so readily. There had to be some other explanation.

"Jun is not here," she said, drawing herself up again, "and we have not heard from him, either. I'm afraid we can't help you."

The man was not put off. "There *is* one matter you can assist us with," he said. "Your son's last report before he left—it included a message addressed to Min. I believe that's your daughter?"

A shock went through me when he said my name.

"I have been sent here to show it to her. It may offer clues to Jun's location—or the Pearl's. Perhaps he wrote it in a code language only she would understand."

"Again, I think you have the wrong impression of my son," Mom said haughtily. "He is an honorable soldier, not a traitor."

"So you say. But I am not leaving these premises until I have shown Min the message. Are you not curious to see his last communication?"

That did the trick.

"Min!" Mom called.

TWO

I ducked back around the corner before she could spot me, waited a couple moments, then walked out to greet them both. My nose tickled again, and I stifled a sneeze. "Yes, Mom?" I asked, pretending I hadn't been eavesdropping on their conversation.

Mom briefly explained the situation to me. "This man has a message from Jun," she said. "He'd like you to tell him if you see anything unusual in it." I could hear the skepticism in her voice.

I nodded sullenly at the investigator, resenting the fact that he had accused Jun of deserting. Still, there was a silver lining: the man seemed unaware that we were foxes.

"Please, let me see the message," I said, remembering to speak formally.

The investigator looked down at me. If I'd been in fox shape, my ears would have flattened against my skull. His expression wasn't condescending, as I would have expected. Instead, I could sense him measuring me. And now I could smell some suspicion coming off him. Did he think I was hiding something?

He drew a data-slate out of a pocket, tapped on it, and

showed me a message marked with Jun's seal—nothing fancy, just his name done in simple calligraphy.

I scowled at the fact that they'd been snooping into my brother's private correspondence, but there was nothing I could do about it now.

> *Hello Min,*
>
> > *Don't tell Bora, but there are even more chores on a battle cruiser than there are at home. I can't wait until my first leave. I have so many things to tell you. I've made lots of friends. Together we've been exploring a new world, just like Dad. My friends help with the chores sometimes, too. Did I mention the chores?*
> >
> > *Love,*
> > *Jun*

I blinked rapidly. I wasn't going to cry, not in front of this stranger. I handed the slate to Mom so she could read it, too. Jun's letters to us had been few and far between. The Thousand Worlds lacked faster-than-light communication technology, so all interstellar messages had to be delivered by courier. I couldn't bear the idea that this might be the last we ever heard from my brother. The investigator had to be wrong.

Still, the message's contents gave me hope. There *was* a hidden meaning in there, all right. Jun had never complained about chores the whole time we were growing up. He was trying to tell me that something was wrong. Who were the "friends"? Were they really friends, or troublemakers he'd fallen in with? Why hadn't he included any of their names?

The most worrying clue was his mention of Dad. For one

thing, our dad had died seven years ago, when I was six. And for another, he had never been an explorer. According to Mom, he'd been a skilled technician. What was Jun trying to imply?

How much of this did I want to reveal to the investigator, though? I didn't trust the man. After all, I didn't know anything about him or his motives. On the other hand, I couldn't thwart him too obviously. That might get my family in trouble, and if he decided to investigate us further, our secret—that we were fox spirits—might be exposed.

I'd hesitated too long. "Min," the investigator said in a disturbingly quiet voice, "can you tell me anything about this?"

"He's just complaining," I said, doing my best not to sound grudging—or concerned.

His gaze captured mine. "That's not the whole story, is it?"

I wasn't going to rat Jun out to some stranger. "I don't know what you mean."

I smelled an extra whiff of worry from Mom. She wanted me to do something in response, but what?

"Many powerful people are interested in the Dragon Pearl," the investigator said, as if I couldn't have guessed that. "If it has resurfaced, it is imperative that it be recovered by the Space Forces and not some unscrupulous person."

I understood why that was important. According to legend, the Pearl could transform an entire planet in a day. Dragons controlled terraforming magic, but they were not nearly that fast and efficient—it took years for teams of trained workers to make a world fully lush and hospitable. As a citizen of Jinju, I was especially aware of that fact. Jun was, too.

With a sinking feeling, I remembered why Jun had wanted to go into the Space Forces. *I want to learn how to help Jinju, to make life better for everyone here,* he had told me more than once.

He wouldn't have stolen the Pearl for *our* benefit, would he? Surely not.

"I don't know anything," I said quickly.

The investigator looked dubious.

Fortunately, Mom intervened. "I assure you, my son would never desert, and my daughter is telling the truth."

I was grateful to her for supporting us and shutting him down.

Then she surprised me by adding, "Perhaps you would like some refreshments before heading to your next stop?"

I suppressed a groan. I didn't want this man here any longer than necessary. Not even Charm could disguise the modesty of our dome house. I tried to remember how well I'd wiped down the lacquered dining table that we brought out for special occasions. All our other furniture was scratched, banged-up plastic. Great-Grandmother had brought the red-black table and its accompanying red silk cushions when she immigrated to Jinju. Mom was going to make me drag it all out for this horrible man who thought Jun had done something wrong.

The man cocked his eyebrows at Mom. I bristled. I bet he doubted we had anything good to offer him. The thing was, we didn't. But Mom had invited him, which made him a guest, which meant I had to treat him politely.

"I'll stay for a meal," he said, as if he were doing *us* a favor. "We can discuss matters further."

"Min," Mom said with a sigh, "get the table ready. You know the one."

"Yes, Mom," I said. She meant the nice table. I had a better idea, though. Especially since I was dying to know what else the investigator had to say about Jun.

On the way to the dining area that adjoined the kitchen, I passed the common room, where my four aunties were still huddled in bed. "Privilege of age," they always said about their sleeping late. Of course when I tried lazing about, I got cuffed on the side of the head. Not hard, but it still infuriated me.

Once I reached the kitchen, I grabbed settings out of cupboards and drawers and laid them out on the counter: chopsticks, spoons, and bowls for rice, soup, and the small side dishes called banchan, like mung bean sprouts and gimchi, spicy pickled cabbage. I grabbed real rice, imported from off-world and saved for special occasions because it required too much water to grow, instead of the crumbly altered grains we produced locally. After hesitating, I added some of the fancier foods and drinks we saved for festival days, like honey cookies and cinnamon-ginger punch. As I worked, I tried to listen in as Mom and the stranger talked in the hallway, but their voices were too low.

"I'm just about done, Mom!" I called out so she'd know to bring the guest in.

Then I concentrated hard, thinking about rectangles, right angles, and straight lines. About the smooth, polished red-black surface of that lacquer table. If I was going to imitate a table, I had to appear better than the real thing.

Charm swirled and eddied around me. My shape wavered, then condensed into that of the knee-high table. I couldn't put out the table settings now—Mom would have to take care of that. In the meantime, while I could only observe the room as a blur through the reflections on my surface, I could listen pretty well.

Most foxes only used shape-shifting to pass as humans in ordinary society. My true form, which I hadn't taken since I was a small child, was that of a red fox. I had one single tail instead of the nine that the oldest and most powerful fox spirits did. Even Great-Grandmother, before she'd passed several years ago, had only had three tails in her fox shape. When the aunties had told us stories about magic and supernatural creatures, and taught us lore about our powers, they had cautioned us to avoid shifting into inanimate objects. It was too easy to become dazed and forget how to change back into a living creature, they'd warned. I'd experimented with it on the sly, though, and was confident I could pull it off.

I heard footsteps. Mom's I would have recognized anywhere. She had a soft way of walking. The investigator also stepped quietly—too quietly, almost like a predator. Like a fox.

"Where did your daughter go off to?" the investigator asked.

A flicker told me that Mom was looking at the countertop where I'd left the settings out. "Pardon her flightiness," she said with a trace of annoyance. "She's been like that a lot lately."

Is that so? I thought.

Mom began transferring the dishes onto my surface. I endured the weird sensation of being a piece of furniture. Even as a table, I had a keen sense of smell—a side effect of being a fox. The rich aroma of cinnamon-ginger punch would have made my mouth water if I'd been in human form. It didn't always work in my favor, though. The cabbage pickles were starting to go sour. I bet the investigator would be able to tell.

Clunk, clunk, clunk went the dishes as they landed on my surface. Mom wasn't slamming them down, but they sounded loud. Then she put the silk cushions on the floor for the courier and her to sit on.

I had a sudden urge to sneeze, which felt very peculiar as a table. It wasn't my own Charm causing it—

Mom?

I concentrated to get a better picture of what Mom was up to. I was right—she was using more Charm! And this time she wasn't doing it to fancy up her clothes. Rather, her Charm was focused on the investigator, who still hadn't given his name. She was trying to get him to lower his guard, by using the kind of magic she had always told me honorable foxes never resorted to. The prickling sensation intensified, although it wasn't directed at me.

I quivered with outrage. Some of the platters on my surface clanked. The investigator froze in the middle of reaching for his chopsticks. "What was that?" he asked.

"Maybe there was a tremor," Mom said after a brief pause. "We get those from time to time." I could smell her suppressed anger, even if she was hiding it from the investigator. She was onto me. I was going to be lectured later, I just knew it.

Surely the investigator wouldn't fall for her excuse? This region was old and quiet, no volcanoes or anything. But I resolved to tamp down my reactions.

"You must have traveled a great distance to reach us here in the outer rim," Mom said. "I'm sorry I can't be more helpful in the matter about my son. Serving in the Space Forces was his dream, you know. I can't imagine that he'd turn his back on it."

His voice was curt. "Your daughter's hiding something, Ms. Kim. If you don't help me determine what it is, then I will be forced to open a general investigation into your family. In my experience, everyone has dirty laundry. Even in a place like Jinju."

He didn't get any further. I wasn't going to let him get away with threatening my mom! Especially since our family did, in fact, have a secret we couldn't afford to reveal. My senses jumbled as I resumed human shape. I shook the dishes off my back. But I hadn't reckoned on getting burned by hot soup as it splashed out of upturned bowls. I yelped. My flailing caused more of the dishes to crash on the floor and break. I was going to have kitchen cleanup duty for the rest of my life.

"Min!" my mom shouted. She attempted to grab my arm and yank me out of there.

I dodged her, flung a shard at the man, and scooted backward. I didn't want to get too close, because he was a lot bigger and it would've been easy for him to overpower me. On the other hand, I wasn't going to run away and leave my mom alone with him.

Mom made another grab for me. "This is *not* the way," she said in a taut voice. "Let me handle it."

It was too late. The investigator and I locked gazes. "Foxes," he hissed. His eyes had gone hard and intense, like a predator's. Even with the gimchi dumped over his head and dripping down the bridge of his nose, he looked threatening. I could smell the anger rising off him. "So *that's* why they needed the cadet."

Before I could react, he lunged for me and snatched me up by the throat. I scrabbled for air, my fingernails lengthening into claws, and tore desperately at his fingers.

"Please," Mom said, low and fast. "I'll make her tell you anything you need to know. Just let her go."

"You're in no position to bargain, Ms. Kim," he said. "Do you realize how bad it will look that one of your kind joined the Space Forces only to go rogue? Or how paranoid the local population will become when they realize that anyone they know could be a fox in disguise? I have no choice but to inform the authorities about your presence here." He reached into his coat, and his fingers closed around something that gleamed.

I panicked, thinking he was going to draw a blaster. I turned into the densest, heaviest block of metal I could manage. Gravity yanked me straight down onto the man's foot. Mom sneezed in response to my shape-shifting magic. The investigator didn't scream or even grunt, just remained silent. That scared me most of all.

Making rapid changes exhausted me, but what choice did I have? The world swam around me as I took human shape again. My clothes tugged awkwardly at my elbows and knees. I'd gotten the garments' measurements wrong.

Gray-faced, the man bent over to examine his foot. Before he stood upright again, I snatched up a saucepan and brought it crashing down against his head. He fell without a sound.

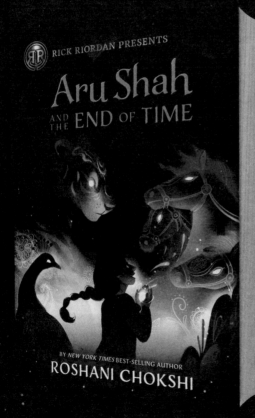

ROSHANI CHOKSHI is the author of the instant *New York Times* best-selling novel *The Star-Touched Queen* and its companion, *A Crown of Wishes*. She studied fairy tales in college, and she has a pet luck dragon that looks suspiciously like a Great Pyrenees dog. *Aru Shah and the End of Time*, her middle grade debut, was inspired by the stories her grandmother told her, as well as Roshani's all-consuming love for *Sailor Moon*. She lives in Georgia and says "y'all," but she doesn't really have a Southern accent, alas. For more information, visit her website, www.roshanichokshi.com, or follow her on Twitter @Roshani_Chokshi.

J. C. CERVANTES grew up in San Diego, California, near the Tijuana border, where she discovered her fascination for Maya and Aztec mythologies. Now she lives with her husband, Joseph, in New Mexico, which has many more volcanoes than most people think. She is the mother of three daughters, the youngest of whom inspired her critically acclaimed first novel, *Tortilla Sun*. Her wish is that children everywhere see themselves reflected in the pages of the books that inspire them and learn to see beyond their own lives, recognizing and celebrating others. She believes in magic, always roots for the underdog, and eats salsa with nearly every meal. For more information, go to www.jennifercervantes.com or follow her on Twitter (@jencerv) and Instagram (authorjcervantes).

YOON HA LEE is a Korean American who grew up in both Texas and South Korea, learning folktales of wily foxes, shape-shifting tigers, and benevolent dragons. Yoon was inspired to write about foxes in space because everything is better in space—except the ice cream. Yoon is also the author of the Machineries of Empire trilogy: *Ninefox Gambit*, *Raven Stratagem*, and *Revenant Gun*. For more information, follow Yoon on Twitter @motomaratai.

RICK RIORDAN, dubbed "storyteller of the gods" by *Publishers Weekly*, is the author of five *New York Times* #1 best-selling series, including *Magnus Chase and the Gods of Asgard*, based on Norse myths. He is best known for his Percy Jackson and the Olympians books, which bring Greek mythology to life for contemporary readers. He expanded on that series with two more: the *Heroes of Olympus* and the *Trials of Apollo*, which cleverly combine Greek and Roman gods and heroes with his beloved modern characters. Rick tackled the ancient Egyptian gods in the magic-filled Kane Chronicles trilogy. Millions of fans across the globe have enjoyed his fast-paced and funny quest adventures as well as his two #1 best-selling myth collections, *Percy Jackson's Greek Gods* and *Percy Jackson's Greek Heroes*. Rick is also the publisher of an imprint at Disney Hyperion, Rick Riordan Presents, dedicated to finding other authors of highly entertaining fiction based on world cultures and mythologies. He lives in Boston, Massachusetts, with his wife and two sons. For more information, go to www.rickriordan.com, or follow him on Twitter @camphalfblood.